# Mail Order Mayhem

Book one in the Brides of Beckham
Kirsten Osbourne

# Chapter One

New England, 1883

Maude picked at her dinner, wishing her parents hadn't invited Horace Templeton for Sunday dinner yet again. He seemed to think he was coming to dinner because he was courting her, but she had no interest in being courted by a man twenty years her senior who looked at her as if she were going to be on his plate for breakfast. He kept casting her sly glances as if to say he knew something she didn't.

Maude didn't consider herself a raving beauty by any means. She was short, with raven colored hair and large gray eyes. She'd turned nineteen just six short weeks before, and her parents were starting to worry their only child would never marry. Of course, her father found a way to find fault with every young man who had ever expressed an interest in her, so she wasn't sure why they were concerned. If he would just slack off, maybe things would be different.

Since Maude was a child, her mother, Lillian Abernathy, had volunteered at a local orphanage three afternoons a week. As soon as she finished her schooling, Maude had joined her mother, and worked there six days per week. She enjoyed working with the children and helping out there. She didn't feel the need to marry right away as her few friends had. She was willing to take her time to find someone who was right for her, even if it meant being an old maid at twenty.

After dinner, she immediately stood to help her mother clear away the dishes from the table. Their only servant didn't work in the evenings, and she and her mother stacked the dishes in the sink for the maid to wash in the mornings.

Lilly shook her head at Maude. "Why don't you take our guest into the parlor and keep him company while I finish up with the dishes?" Her eyes pleaded with Maude to not make a scene and spend time with the man.

Maude looked toward her father waiting for him to get up and head to the parlor first. He remained seated. "I think I'm going to have a second piece of pie and a cup of coffee. You go on." He waved his hand toward the door indicating they should go without him.

Her parents had never left her alone with any man in her entire life, so she knew something was wrong. Why would they want her to be alone with him, when they wouldn't allow her to be alone with any other man?

Maude led the way to the parlor hating how closely Mr. Templeton followed her. She'd known him all her life and he'd made her uncomfortable for years. She carefully took a seat in one of the chairs and left the settee for him, so he couldn't sit too closely as he was wont to do. Once they were seated, she gave him her full attention. She struggled for a topic she could use to begin a conversation with him. "How is business at the bank, Mr. Templeton?"

He ignored her question, and instead got to the topic that was on his mind. "Please, call me Horace." He waited for a moment, and then leaned forward to take her hand in his. "I spoke with your father this morning, and he agreed that I may ask you to marry me." His eyes were intense and she felt a shudder run down her spine. She couldn't marry him. He made her too jittery.

She sat looking down at her hands, unsure how to respond. He hadn't really asked her anything, so she chose not to respond at all, but kept looking down, not meeting his eyes. Hopefully he would take the hint and drop the subject.

"Well?" He didn't even try to keep the annoyance out of his voice.

"Well what?"

"Are you going to answer my question?"

"I'm sorry, sir. I wasn't aware you'd asked one. It sounded more like a statement to me." She knew she was annoying him, but she didn't want to marry him, but didn't want to come right out and say so.

He sighed. "I forget how young you are." He shook his head at her as if it was a crime to be young. "Will you marry me?" Although worded as a question, it came out as more of a demand than anything else.

She closed her eyes and took a deep breath. "No, thank you." The words were whispered, but audible nonetheless.

"Your father has already agreed on your behalf." His voice was mild as he informed her of her future. She had no choice in the matter as far as he was concerned. Her only hope was that her parents would see how she felt about it.

She looked up at him to see his eyes glinting with anger. What was it about this man that frightened her so much? She'd never been particularly shy or afraid of men. It was just him. He made her skin feel like there were a million spiders crawling across it. "So why did you ask me if you already had your answer?" She kept the anger and fear from her voice and asked the question as if she were merely curious.

He shrugged. "I just wanted to make you feel like you had a choice. Of course, you don't, but every girl should feel like she has a choice in life." He stood, pulling her to her feet with the hand that was still holding hers. He leaned down and kissed her then, forcing his tongue into her mouth.

Horace was an older man who'd let himself go to pot over the years. He was almost as wide as he was tall and had brown hair liberally dusted with gray. At least what little hair he had left was liberally dusted with gray. The touch of his lips on hers made her want to vomit, and it was everything she could do not to pull away from him.

He smelled as if he hadn't bathed in months, and his hair was so oily, she was certain she could fix the hinges on the front door with it. He was no one's idea of a matrimonial prize. She would speak to her father after he left and let him know in no uncertain terms she would not be marrying this man.

Finally, he let her go and leered down at her in a manner that made her want to add an overcoat and a blanket to her perfectly modest dress to cover herself better. It was as if he were trying to see right through her clothing. He actually looked at her as if he was expecting her to jump on him with uncontrollable passion. She did her best to swallow the vomit threatening to escape. She wished he'd asked her when her stomach was empty.

"Let's go tell your parents the happy news!" He pulled her after him into the dining room where her parents were waiting. Her mother had an anxious look on her face, like she knew Maude wouldn't want to marry the man, but would be afraid to say anything against it. Her father's face glowed making Maude wonder what he'd been offered to give his only child to the hideous man beside her.

"Maude has agreed to be my wife." Horace's voice was filled with pride as he spoke the words as if it was his magnificent physique that had turned the young woman's head.

Maude didn't say anything, because Horace's words were anything but true. She'd never agreed to anything. She wouldn't marry him if she had to run away with a wagon train going west. She just couldn't do it. He repulsed her and she wouldn't say otherwise.

Morgan Abernathy got to his feet, his face filled with delight. He hugged his Maude tightly. "I'm so happy for you, dear!" He looked over at Lilly. "Aren't you happy?"

Lilly looked slightly horrified, but nodded quickly. "Yes, of course. When will you be married, Mr. Templeton?" Maude watched her mother's face knowing if she could get one of her parents to see things her way, it would be her mother.

Horace sat at the table in the same spot he'd recently vacated. He refused to sit anywhere but the head of the table no matter where he was. "I need to leave tomorrow on business and will be gone for approximately three months. I need to travel to New York City. I would like to be married as soon after my return as possible."

Lilly nodded. "Why don't we plan the wedding for four months from now?" She had a piece of paper in front of her on the table. She picked up the pen and dipped it in the ink and very carefully wrote. "Do you have any requirements for the wedding?"

Horace shrugged. "That's women's work. All I care about is getting married." He gave Maude another look that made her feel slightly queasy. How could anyone possibly think that a woman her age would be interested in him? The only thing he had going for him was money, but that wasn't enough to offset his bad points, and Maude had never cared much about money anyway.

Lilly smiled at him. "Maude and I will work out the details together while you're away then. I'll talk to our pastor and see when we can use the church in that time frame, and we'll give you the time and date."

"That sounds fine. I need to leave in the morning, so I should be going. Maude, you'll walk me to the door." Again it was a command that left no room for argument.

Maude followed him meekly to the door, but inside she was furious. How could her parents expect her to marry a hideous old man? Why could they possibly think it was in her best interests to do so? Her stomach heaved at the idea of sleeping in a bed with him.

At the front door, he turned to her and pulled her into his arms, leaning down to kiss her again. His hand slid around her side and up her corset. She stood still letting him touch her, knowing she would never submit to marriage to him. No matter what, she was not going to spend the rest of her life with this terrible man.

Finally he tore himself away and smiled down at her. "I'll hurry back so you don't have to worry that you'll have time to miss that too much. I can't wait to make you my wife." He winked at her as if he knew that depriving her of his touch would be horrible for her.

She didn't return his smile, simply staring at him. "Good night, Mr. Templeton."

He laughed. "We're going to be married. You need to start calling me Horace." He opened the door and walked out into the fresh spring air.

As she watched him leave, she felt resentment growing inside her. She walked straight to the dining room where her parents were sitting.

"I'm not marrying him!" The words came out much louder and more shrilly than she'd meant them to. She hadn't meant to scream, but she'd kept so much bottled up while dealing with Mr. Templeton that she couldn't keep it in a moment longer. "How could you even agree to let him ask me?"

Her father stood. "You have no other marriage prospects. Of course, you'll marry him. He's rich, and he'll provide well." His look was hard. "You have no choice."

"I want to marry a man whom I can love! Not some old man who makes my skin crawl! He's dirty and he smells bad." She looked to her mother for help, but Lilly just sat with her head hung, not meeting Maude's eyes.

Morgan took a step closer to Maude, squeezing her chin between his fingers as he forced her eyes to his. "I've let your mother handle you for too long. You will be an obedient daughter and marry him. Go to bed."

Maude ran from the room with tears streaming down her face. She ran to her room, wrenching the door open and slamming it loudly behind her. Throwing herself across her bed, she wept loudly. "I won't marry him. They can't make me!"

# Chapter Two

During the following week, Maude found herself a lot more aware of her surroundings. She was constantly looking for an escape from her situation. On Wednesday, she walked into the post office on her way home from the orphanage, to see if they'd received any mail. The woman in line in front of her was chatting with the clerk about the handful of letters she'd just received. "I don't think I have enough women to fill all these requests! I've only had five sign up, but there are at least ten letters here."

The clerk smiled. The two were obviously friends. "I'm surprised you were able to find even five women willing to be mail order brides. I can't imagine marrying someone I'd never met. A woman would have to be truly desperate to do that." She shook her head, looking horrified at the prospect of being a mail order bride.

Maude couldn't help but chime into the conversation. "You mean like being told you have to marry a man more than twice your age who smells badly and is hideous? Is that the kind of desperate you mean?" Her voice had a hint of panic to it as she asked the question and the other two women gave their full attention to her.

The first woman, who was clutching the letters, turned in the line and looked at her. "That's exactly the kind of desperate you need to be." She paused, her warm brown eyes meeting Maude's blue. "I'm Harriett. When's the wedding?" Her voice was sympathetic as she took Maude's hand in hers and squeezed it.

Maude looked down. "Four months, but he'll be back in three, and I want to be gone before he gets here. I want to be gone in two months or less if at all possible."

Harriett nodded and smiled. "That's more than enough time. Let me buy you a slice of pie."

The postmistress handed Maude a letter without saying a word. She'd watched her sad eyes every day as she'd come to get the mail. Maude had never been one to talk much with her, but she knew something was very wrong.

Maude followed Harriett out of the post office and to the restaurant next door. It was a small place, with only six tables. Maude had never been here before, but her parents didn't often take her out to eat. She'd only been to a restaurant a couple of times in her life. She took a seat across from Harriett and sighed heavily. "I can't marry him."

Harriett smiled at her, squeezing her hand. "You won't have to." She fanned the letters out for Maude. "Let's read these and we'll pick the very best one for you." Harriett picked up one and opened it while Maude did the same.

As the waitress came and went, leaving their pie and some coffee, the two women read letter after letter. Each made a pile of rejects and their favorites. When they'd opened them all, Harriett gave her full attention to Maude again. "I know which one I'd pick, but what about you? What are you looking for?"

Maude shrugged. "I really didn't think I was in a big hurry to marry. I haven't thought about it much, but I do know what I don't want." A picture formed in her mind of Horace's sweaty face with his eyes gleaming at her. "I know exactly what I don't want."

Harriett held up two letters. "These are my favorites. This one is a farmer and needs a wife. He has never been married and has no children. He lives in Iowa." She wiggled the other letter. "This one is a widower. He has two small children and owns a general store in a small town in Minnesota. He lost his wife to Scarlet Fever just a few months ago, and needs someone to help him with his little ones."

The letter Maude was holding was from a man in Washington Territory who worked as a lumberjack. "I think I like yours better than mine." She took the two letters from Harriett's hands and read them carefully. The man in Iowa was named John Powers. He wrote with a neat hand and talked about his farm and how badly he needed a wife to help him with it. The man in Minnesota was Benjamin Johnson, and he spoke of his two small girls, ages four and six, and their need for a mother.

She sat looking at them both unfolded on the table in front of her and finally she looked up at Harriett. "I think I want to marry John. I love children, but I'd rather have my own than take care of someone else's." She wouldn't have a problem with Benjamin either, though. She would happily marry either of them rather than stay here and marry Horrible Horace.

Harriett nodded. "I'd feel that way myself. Write to him." She pushed the letter back across the table to Maude and put the others in a neat pile.

Maude smiled. "I will. Anything to get out of marrying Horace." She took another bite of her apple pie, sighing happily as the flavors exploded on her tongue. There was nothing Maude liked better than apple pie, and this one was baked to perfection.

Harriett's eyes widened. "Not Horace Templeton? The bank owner?"

"That's him."

Harriett let out a little shudder. "That man is not right in his head. One of the other women, who is looking for a husband, used to be a maid in his house. The stories that woman told would make your hair curl." She straightened. "We're going to make this work. You keep your head down and act like everything is okay. Make whatever wedding plans you need to make, but don't be alone with him. Promise me that."

Maude nodded. "As I said, he's out of town on business for the next three months. I'd like to be gone well before he returns."

"That would be best. We'll hurry. Write that letter today, and we'll get it done." Her face was filled with fear for Maude. Maude was afraid to ask just what Harriett knew about Horace, though. She knew she was better off not knowing.

Harriett promised she would be outside the post office at four in the afternoon as soon as a letter was received. Maude couldn't risk someone else getting the mail, so she had the letter sent to Harriett. Maude sighed with relief as she had a plan to get away from her marriage to Horace the horrid.

When Maude returned home that afternoon, she immediately closed herself into her bedroom to write her response to John. Her message was short and to the point. "Hello, John. My name is Maude, and I'm nineteen years old. I live in the city of Beckham, which is near Boston, with my parents. I would love to come west to be your wife. I am short with dark hair and blue eyes. I hope to meet you soon. I will be ready to leave as soon as I receive word from you. All the best, Maude."

She tucked the letter into the pocket of her skirt and went to speak with her mother. "I need to run and meet a friend for a moment. Do you have any errands that need to be done while I'm out?"

Her mother eyed her skeptically. "You're not meeting a young man are you?" Maude had never been one to meet young men, but she'd also never been engaged before, and she'd never just run off to do errands.

Maude shook her head. "Of course not, Mother. I'm an engaged woman now." Her eyes met her mother's and she tried to convey her acceptance of the situation, even as she clutched the letter she'd written John in the pocket of her skirt.

"I know Mr. Templeton isn't the man you've always wanted to marry, but your father and I feel he'll do well for you. You'll live in comfort for the rest of your life." Lilly bit her lip as she waited for her daughter's explosion of anger. "You'll have servants waiting to fulfill your every request. Your life will be a dream."

Maude hugged her mother. "I understand."

Maude quickly walked to the post office to mail off the letter. She asked how long it would take for a letter to reach Iowa as she handed it to the postmistress. "About two weeks." The woman gave her a pitying look that told her she knew just why she and Harriett had left together. Maude kept her head high as she left the post office.

Two weeks each way. So if he received the letter and responded on the same day, it would be a minimum of a month before she had any sort of response. She sucked in a breath. She'd have to go along with all the wedding plans. Her mother was working on a wedding dress for her, and a trousseau was being made. She would go along with all the plans, and just use everything for her wedding to John.

# Chapter Three

The month flew by with her wedding preparations. Maude and Lilly addressed over a hundred wedding invitations. As she rubbed her sore hand from all the writing, she felt guilty about sending out invitations to a wedding that would never take place, but she told herself she had no choice. She couldn't marry Horace. She simply couldn't.

Exactly four weeks and two days after she'd mailed her letter to John, she saw Harriett in the post office. Their eyes met and Harriett gave a slow nod, letting her know she'd received the letter. They left the building and once again went to the restaurant next door for pie and coffee. As they sat, Harriett handed Maude the letter.

"Hello Maude. I'm pleased you are willing to travel all this way to be my bride. I'm enclosing a train ticket for Monday, May seventh and some funds for any expenses you have on your trip. I will wait for you at the train depot, and drive you to Hudspeth where we will be married by my pastor that afternoon. I've made all the arrangements. I look forward to meeting you. Yours, John."

Maude's hand shook as she read the letter and put it down on the table. "That's only three days from now!" She did a mental inventory of what she'd need to pack, nervous now that the day to leave Beckham was so close.

Harriett nodded. "It's moving fast, but that's what we wanted for you." She reached over and squeezed Maude's hand in hers. "I know it's scary to get on a train knowing you'll be marrying someone you've never met on the other end, but there's really no choice."

"I'll need to get the things I want to take with me ready. I've had a small bag packed all along, but I'll need to pack one more. Would you be willing to meet me to keep them for me?"

"Of course! Where do you live?" The town of Beckham, Massachusetts was not large by any means, but large enough that you certainly didn't know everyone who lived there like you would in a small town.

Maude quickly gave her address, and they agreed to meet at midnight just down the street from Maude's home that night. Harriett would meet her at the train station Monday morning with her things. "Thank you so much! I don't know what I would have done if we hadn't met in the post office that day."

"You'd have found some other way out." Harriett smiled at her new friend. "I can see you're a strong woman, and you wouldn't have married him."

They walked quietly through the streets toward Maude's home. When they were a few houses away, they hugged quickly with a promise to meet that night.

Maude went straight to her room and packed for her trip. She couldn't leave her closet bare in case her mother went in there, so she packed just two everyday dresses plus her pale pink wedding dress she would be able to use as a church dress once she'd arrived in Iowa. She didn't know how practical it would be for a farmer's wife to have a silk Sunday dress, but it didn't really matter. She wasn't going to leave it behind. She stowed her bags under her bed and went down to meet her mother.

Lilly looked up with a smile as Maude walked into the dining room where she was seated at the table working on something. "Oh good! I was hoping you'd help me with the menu for the wedding."

Maude sat with her mother and discussed the merits of chicken over beef all the while knowing she wouldn't be attending the elaborate wedding her mother was planning. She wished she could confess to her mother what she'd done, but she was too afraid. She couldn't let anything keep her from leaving Beckham. She would write a letter of apology once she was married.

At five minutes before midnight, Maude opened her bedroom door as softly as she could, hoping to not wake her parents. She tiptoed to their bedroom door, and put her ear to the door. All she could hear was her father snoring. He never went to bed before her mother, so she was certain she was safe. She went back into her bedroom, and opened her window, dropping her bags out. There was nothing breakable in them. She'd packed nothing with any sentimental value, only a few books and her clothing.

She looked out the window. She'd once climbed down the tree that was just outside it when she was younger, but decided that would be too risky. She tiptoed down the stairs and out the front door, going to the side of the house to pick up her bags. She moved quickly down the street she'd lived on her entire life wondering what it would be like to live somewhere else. To not know every neighbor. To not have her mother's face across the table from her every morning.

Harriett was waiting and took the bags from her. "Did you have any trouble getting out?"

"No, my parents are both asleep. I threw the bags out my window just in case one of them woke up and saw me. I could say I couldn't sleep and was going for a walk."

Harriett nodded in the darkness. "That was a good idea. Well, I'll see you Monday morning at the train station."

"Thank you!"

"You're welcome, Maude. I'm happy to help you!"

Maude didn't breathe deeply again until she was in her bedroom with the door closed and back in her nightgown. The riskiest part of the entire plan was over. She always spent Monday mornings at the orphanage, so it wouldn't surprise anyone when she left for the train. She wouldn't even be questioned.

MAUDE SLOWLY SIPPED her milk as she toyed with the eggs on her plate Monday morning. Her mother looked at her with concern. "You're not eating? Are you starting to get pre-wedding jitters?"

Maude almost laughed out loud. Yes, she was getting pre-wedding jitters, but for her wedding with John, not with Horace. Horace had only inspired pre-wedding nightmares. "A little. It'll be strange to not live here with you and Father. I've never lived anywhere else." She'd never slept anywhere but her own bed.

Lilly smiled encouragingly. "It's the natural order of things. You grow up and you marry. You'll enjoy being in charge of your own home. And you'll have plenty of servants to help you adjust."

Maude just shrugged, knowing there would be no servants for her. Thankfully she'd learned to cook and take care of small children at the orphanage. Her parents had raised her with no real skills except playing the piano, and that would do her no good at all on a farm in Iowa. All the homemaking skills she had were learned from her volunteer hours at the orphanage.

Her father looked up from his morning paper. "I got word Friday that Mr. Templeton will be home this coming Sunday. He was able to finish up his business early. We'll have him over for Sunday dinner and you'll be polite and make it clear to him you want to be his wife."

She nodded. "Yes, Father." Inside she felt a moment of panic. He was coming home early. She was making it out just in time. She forced herself to breathe steadily. She just had to make it to the train station, and she was gone. They would have no way of finding her.

She looked around her as she made the short walk to the train station. She hated the thought of leaving this beautiful little city so close to the Atlantic Ocean. She woke up in the morning smelling the sea air. *What would Iowa smell like?*

She took her time walking, knowing the train wouldn't leave for another hour. It was strange knowing she was walking the streets of Beckham for the last time. She'd said goodbye to her parents as if she were leaving for the day, but inside, she'd known she was leaving for good. *Dear God, please let John be a better man than Horace!*

Harriett was waiting with her bags at the train station. She took them from her friend and held the ticket in her hand. It would take four days to reach Iowa, so she would be meeting John on Friday, and having her wedding Friday afternoon. "Promise me you'll write as soon as you get there."

Maude smiled at her friend. "I will. Thank you so much for all your help. I don't know how I'd have gotten away without you. I'll keep in touch."

Harriett hugged her quickly. "Have a safe trip. I'll be watching for your letter."

Harriett watched as the train headed down the tracks with a loud blow of the whistle. She'd only had her mail order bride business for a couple of months, and Maude was the first bride she'd seen off. She said a silent prayer for her friend, hoping she was off to a better situation than she had here.

# Chapter Four

It was late morning when the train pulled into the station in Ogden, Iowa. Maude felt disgusting after the long train ride. She'd done some spit baths along the way, but more than anything she wanted to soak in a hot bath for hours to get clean. She didn't want to meet John looking like she'd been traveling for days even though she had.

She stepped off the train looking around for a man who looked like he was looking for her. She should have asked him what he looked like, but she hadn't thought of it. Frankly she hadn't cared as long as he wasn't Horace. After a moment, she saw a man holding up a piece of wood with her name painted on it. She headed straight for the sign, searching the face of the man holding it.

He'd mentioned in the first letter that he was in his mid-twenties which seemed like a good age to her. He was a tall man, with blond hair. She couldn't see his eye color across the distance, but she was pretty certain they'd be blue or green. As she got closer to him, she held out her hand to shake his. "I'm Maude Abernathy." She was pleased to see he'd dressed in a jacket and tie to meet her and for their wedding. She'd expected a man in dirty britches and suspenders. It was nice to see she was wrong.

He smiled broadly, taking her hand in his and shaking it. "Did you have a good trip?"

"It was tiring, but exciting. This was my first time on a train."

He looked around for her luggage, but didn't see anything. "Where are your things?"

"They were in the baggage car." She led him through the crowd to the large crate with all of the bags for the Ogden, Iowa stop. They waited patiently as a uniformed young man emptied the crate.

After her name was called, he carried her two bags to his wagon and helped her up onto the seat. "It's a two hour drive to Hudspeth. The wedding is at one, and I thought we could eat at the reception. Does that sound good?"

She nodded. "We're having a big wedding?" She was surprised he'd had the time or inclination to plan anything. She'd really expected him to find a pastor or a justice of the peace on the way home, but didn't think anyone would be in attendance for the ceremony.

"My sister-in-law decided that we couldn't just speak our words in front of the pastor. She invited the whole church and planned the reception. It won't be elaborate, but it should make it a bit more special than anything I could have thrown together." He kept watching her out of the corner of his eye as he drove out of the town. Why would a woman who looked like she did have to come all this way to find a husband? Why wouldn't she have just had her pick of all the young men in her hometown?

She smiled at that. "I'm glad." She thought about her wedding dress tucked into one of the bags in the back. "Will I have time to change into the wedding dress I brought?" She really wanted to wear the dress she and her mother had made together. It would make her feel closer to her mother on her wedding day.

"Absolutely. My brother's house will be open to you. It's just a few doors down from the church. My sister-in-law, Anne, will probably beg you to let her do your hair." He glanced over at her. "You have beautiful hair by the way."

"Thank you." She was surprised she didn't feel more nervous around this total stranger she'd be married to in just a few hours. "What is your farm like?" She stared at the countryside as they drove slowly out of the city. She looked forward to a quiet life on a farm.

John seemed like a good man, and she wasn't sorry she'd left Beckham. He was handsome in a rugged sort of way, and she didn't have the overwhelming fear of him she'd had for Horace. She was nervous, of course, because she was about to marry a stranger, but not afraid as she would have been on her wedding day back home.

He shrugged. "It's just a farm. Not too big, but not too small. I grow wheat. I have a couple of cows that I use for milk and a few laying hens for cooking. Not much else right now." He paused for a moment. "I need to warn you now my house is a mess. I meant to clean it, but I just didn't have time with the farm chores. I hope you won't hate me when you see it."

"That's fine. I don't mind cleaning." She had done more than her share of scrubbing floors at the orphanage during the past two years. She certainly wouldn't complain about doing the same in her own home. "Do your parents live near here?" She realized then she knew absolutely nothing about the man beside her other than the fact he was a farmer.

He shook his head. "My brother and I came out here on the orphan train. An older couple took us in. They needed help with their farm and in exchange provided us with a home and an education."

"How old were you?"

"Eleven. My brother was thirteen. Our dad was killed during the war." His voice held an air of sadness as he mentioned his father.

"I'm sorry." She didn't ask about his mother, knowing that many children had been put on the train by their mothers when they couldn't afford to care for them. "Where are you from?"

"New York City. I love it here, though. The fresh air, the open land. It's the most wonderful place God created."

She looked around her, taking a deep sniff of the air. It didn't smell like the ocean, and she knew she'd miss that, but she would have someone kind to be with. "I've always lived near the ocean. It smells different here." She wrinkled her nose a bit. "It smells more like animal manure here." She studied his profile as she talked. She wouldn't describe him as handsome, not in the traditional sense. His eyes at close range were a dark green. His nose had obviously been broken at some point in time.

As he drove out of the small city to the country, she noticed him sneaking glances at her. She'd always felt like she was odd looking with her almost black hair and her pale blue eyes. She wondered what he thought of her. "Why didn't you marry some man back in Massachusetts? You're a pretty girl. I'm sure there were men asking to court you all the time."

She shrugged. "My father didn't like any of the men who asked to court me. I never really felt like I was in a hurry to marry. My life was full with my volunteer work." She purposely left out the information about Horace. How would he feel knowing she was engaged to marry two different men? She'd taken off her ring and left it under her pillow at home, knowing someone would find it.

He nodded. "What type of work did you do? You didn't mention it in your letter."

"I volunteered at a local orphanage." She smiled thinking of the children there. "I worked there after school from the time I was fifteen. After I graduated, I went on to working there full time."

"So you like children?" His voice sounded hopeful as he asked that question.

"Oh, yes. I love them. I'd like a whole houseful."

He took her hand and squeezed it in his. "I'd be happy to help you with that."

She felt the blush creep up her neck and cover her whole face. When he touched her, she felt a tingle run up her spine. It was so different than how she'd felt when Horace had touched her. She cleared her throat, searching for a new topic. "What were your adoptive parents like?"

"They were fine. Strict, but good. They didn't beat us or anything, but they sure expected us to work hard. So we did. They let us go to school in the winter when it didn't interfere with farm chores."

"Do they still live near here?"

He shook his head. "Mr. Gunderson died when I was sixteen. I stayed on and helped Mrs. Gunderson, but she died a few years later. They left me the farm. My brother works in town at the mercantile. He always hated farming and moved to town as soon as he could."

"It sounds like you and your brother are close."

"As close as brothers can be. His wife was the one who insisted I send off for a bride. She said she wanted nieces and nephews to spoil." He smiled down at her as he drove. "They don't have any children yet, but she's in the family way."

"I can't wait to meet them both."

"Anne's been chomping at the bit to meet you since your letter came. Al is excited, but not like Anne is. Of course, Al's pretty laid back. Nothing much gets him riled up." He pointed off into the distance. "That's my farm over there. I wish I could take you to see it now, but we really don't have time."

She strained her eyes looking at the house. It was bigger than she'd expected. She figured she'd end up in a small sod house in the middle of nowhere. The house was made of wood and looked sturdy. She could make out a barn as well. "How much further to town?"

"A few miles. We'll be there in about twenty minutes or so."

She smiled. Twenty minutes wasn't too far to drive if she needed supplies, or just craved some female companionship. Her life wouldn't be nearly as desolate as she'd imagined. "It'll be nice living so close to town."

He nodded. "I like it. I'm close enough to go in when I need to, but not so close my neighbors are constantly banging on my door needing something." He pointed to the right. "Our closest neighbors live over there. They're a family of seven. Five kids. All red heads with freckles. Name's O'Malley. Trust me, you'll know them as soon as you see them."

As they drove into the small town, she looked around her with wide eyes. There was almost nothing there. There were several houses, a general store, and a small church. That was all. "Is there no school? No doctor?"

He shook his head. "The church doubles as the school. No sense in putting up another building when they're never used at the same time. The doc works out of his home."

He stopped the horses in front of a small white house with roses and tulips growing in the yard. He walked around and gave her his hand to help her down. "This is my brother's place."

A young woman with blond hair piled high on her head and dark blue eyes hurried outside. "You must be Maude! I'm so happy to meet you." She threw her arms around Maude and hugged her tightly. "I'm Anne. Let's get you ready for your wedding!" She kept an arm around Maude's shoulders, calling over her shoulder, "Make yourself useful and bring in her bags, John!"

The house was small, but welcoming. Maude inhaled deeply of the scent of fresh cookies. "Something smells good!"

Anne grinned. "I've had a real craving for sweets the last few months." She patted the huge mound of her belly with an affectionate sigh. "Only two months to go."

"Do you want a boy or a girl?"

Anne shrugged. "I'd be happy with either one, but I keep telling Al it's a girl just to get his goat. He thinks you should always have a boy first so he can fight off the suitors of any girl that comes along."

John stepped into the house with Maude's bags. "Where do you want them, Anne?"

"Put them in the spare room." After he set them down, she made a shooing motion with her hand. "Go away for a bit. We're going to get your bride ready." She looked at the clock on her mantle. "We'll see you at the church in thirty minutes."

After he'd left, Anne gave her full attention to Maude. "You've been on that train for days. I had Al heat up some water, so there's a bath ready for you in the spare room." She led her to the bedroom with the bathwater already filled. "Take a quick bath, and I'll fix your hair for you.

We don't have time for you to wash your hair and dry it, so just leave it pinned."

She closed the door after giving her instructions, and Maude breathed a sigh of relief. She undressed quickly wishing she had enough time to wash her hair for her wedding. At least she'd be clean, though, and that was what really mattered.

She bathed hurriedly stepping out of the tub ten minutes after Anne shut the door. She reached into her bag and pulled out the wedding dress she'd carefully folded and wrapped in paper to keep it from wrinkling. She put on fresh undergarments and stepped into the dress her mother had painstakingly sewn for her. She wished her mother could be there to see her marry, but she immediately pushed the thought from her mind.

She couldn't reach the buttons on the back, so she opened the door and called Anne. "Would you help me button up?"

Anne immediately hurried into the room buttoning her quickly. When Maude turned to face her, her eyes were twinkling with excitement. "That shade of pink is just perfect on you. You make a beautiful bride." She pushed Maude into a chair and went to work on her hair. "I thought something simple would be best for the wedding. We don't really have time for anything elaborate."

As she worked with her hair she chatted quickly, talking about all of the women in town, most of who had helped with her wedding supper.

When she was finished, Maude turned to a mirror and looked. Anne had expertly swept her hair into an elegant style, leaving a few loose curls to frame her face. Maude was surprised at the effect. The lack of sleep from the days on the train had given her a fragile look that wasn't at all normal for her, but worked well with the hair. She was amazed at how she looked. She smiled and thanked Anne. "You're going to be a good sister."

Anne grinned. "I have eight brothers, but for the life of them, my parents couldn't give me a sister. I'm so thrilled I'm getting one in you!"

Maude smiled, hugging her new friend. "How much time do we have?"

Anne hurried out of the room to consult the mantle clock. "We're a minute late as it is. We need to hurry over there."

Maude sighed. She really wished her parents could have been there. This was a huge step to take without their knowledge or consent. She didn't feel bad about leaving Horace, but she felt terrible about running off without letting her parents know she was leaving or where she was going. She should have left a note, but was too afraid they'd follow her and put an end to her plans.

"My father is going to give you away. I thought it was better than not having someone to do it for you."

Maude smiled. "Thank you for that. I wasn't looking forward to walking down the aisle by myself in front of so many strangers."

Anne hugged Maude tightly. "Don't think of us as strangers. We're future friends."

# Chapter Five

Maude's heart was pounding so loudly during the minute walk to the church, she was surprised people weren't rushing out of their homes to find out who was beating a drum. Anne walked calmly beside her chattering happily about everything from her preparations for the baby to the wedding supper. Maude knew she was talking to try to steady her nerves, but it wasn't helping, and was actually making her a lot more nervous.

When they reached the church, Anne took a bouquet of flowers that was left on a chair just inside the door and handed them to Maude. She reached up and fussed with Maude's hair for a minute, and then whispered, "You're beautiful. John is going to swallow his tongue." She picked up her own bouquet and the woman who'd been hovering at the back signaled someone to start playing the organ.

As she took short even steps toward the front, Maude thought, *She must be my matron of honor. I didn't even know!* Maude looked to the couple standing next to her. The woman, who had signaled the organist, whispered to her. "I'm Anne's mother, Judy Allen. This is my husband, Harvey."

Maude mumbled softly, "It's nice to meet you."

Harvey Allen held his arm out for Maude to take and slowly walked with her up the aisle. John was waiting at the front with a huge smile on his face, obviously pleased Maude was finally here and they were about to marry. When her hand was placed in John's she felt a quick burst of panic. *What am I thinking? I'm standing here in front of total strangers about to marry a man I met just a few hours ago. I have to get out of here!*

John squeezed her hand as if he realized the panicked thoughts rushing through her mind. His eyes met hers and his steady gaze was all

Maude needed. She smiled tentatively and turned to the pastor, listening to him talk about the importance of marriage.

She never knew later how she was able to give all the right answers at the right times, but apparently she'd done okay, because a few minutes later, the pastor announced they were man and wife and invited John to kiss her.

Maude had only ever been kissed by Horace, and she wasn't looking forward to kissing John in front of all these people. She hoped he didn't try to stick his tongue down her throat as Horace had.

His head lowered to hers slowly, and she closed her eyes as his lips brushed hers softly. Maude was surprised when it was over so quickly, and even more surprised that she wanted it to keep going. She opened her eyes and saw John smiling down at her, and she smiled back feeling more positive about her future than she'd dreamed possible.

They turned to the congregation gathered there and the pastor introduced them as Mr. and Mrs. John Powers. Maude breathed a sigh of relief. Even if her parents were able to find out what had happened and arrived now, it would be too late. She was married.

The wedding supper passed in a blur. She was introduced to so many new people she knew she'd never keep them all straight. Through it all, John was at her side. They ate the meal provided by the ladies of the town, and talked to everyone around them. The only person Maude really wanted to be speaking to was her husband, but she didn't have a chance.

Finally, after two hours of talking to strangers, John took her hand and led her to his wagon. Someone had helpfully stowed her bags in the back, so they didn't have to worry about getting them. Everyone waved as they drove away, toward the house that would be her new home.

A casserole had been given to her for their dinner so she wouldn't need to cook on their wedding day. She held it on her lap as if it would protect her from the unknown. As they left the town for the country roads, she heard herself breathe a sigh of relief.

He glanced at her, speaking for the first time since they'd left the church. "Glad it's over?"

She laughed and nodded. "I know I'm supposed to enjoy being the center of attention on my wedding day, but I don't know any of those people. It just felt strange." She didn't add that she wouldn't have enjoyed being the center of attention even if she had known everyone there.

"I'm sorry. I guess I just assumed you'd want a big wedding, so I arranged it. I probably should have asked you what you wanted. I just didn't have the chance."

"No, this was nice. I'm glad I've at least met everyone." She paused looking out over the pretty prairie. "I liked Anne. I think she and I will be fast friends."

"Anne's a good person. She's really excited to have a sister. She told me it was my duty to marry and provide her with a sister she could be friends with."

Maude couldn't help but grin. "I can just hear her saying that."

He left the main road and drove the narrow path to his farm. "I'm sure you're going to need to make some changes to the house. Do whatever you need. If you need supplies, let me know, and we'll go into town to get them."

She was pleased to hear he didn't mind if she made changes. She loved the idea of setting up her house the way she wanted it. "I'll take stock and see what we need to get. If I'm going to be cooking for you, I'm sure I'll need to get some supplies."

"Anne stocked me up with a lot of things. She said you could at least start with what I have on hand." He paused. "Before you see the house, I'm going to warn you. I tried to get it cleaned up, but I'm just not very good at that type of thing. Anne would have helped me, but with as pregnant as she is, I didn't want her to be doing any heavy cleaning for me when she has to do it all at home already."

Maude wondered if it could possibly be as bad as he was making it out to be. After he helped her down from the wagon, she walked toward the door. He opened it for her and she looked inside. She swallowed hard as she saw the mess. He hadn't exaggerated one bit.

The front door opened up to a large room which was a kitchen, dining room and sitting area combined. She could see the piles of dirty pots and dishes. There was a thick layer of grime on the floor throughout. The sitting room had books and tools of some sort scattered everywhere.

The house was a two story, and she could see the stairs leading to the second floor. "What's up there?" she asked with a smile, trying her best to hide how she felt about the filth. She knew what she'd be doing for a long time to come.

"Why don't you go have a look around? I'll get your bags from the wagon."

She slowly climbed the stairs apprehensive about what she'd see. There were three bedrooms, the largest of which was the messiest. The two smaller bedrooms didn't look as if they'd been touched for years, so they were covered in dust, but they didn't have the same level of chaos as the main bedroom. There were clothes thrown everywhere in the master bedroom. The sheet was filthy, and she knew she wouldn't be sleeping there until she'd changed the sheets and washed the quilt.

The furniture was well made and of quality wood, but the neglect it had seen over the years was obvious. She sighed and immediately began picking up the clothes from the floor. By the time John arrived with her bags, she'd already stripped the bed and had made a pile of things to be washed. She hoped he had spare linens because she wouldn't have time to wash and dry the bedding before nightfall.

She felt the anger wash over her in waves. He'd left this huge mess knowing she was coming to clean it up. Why couldn't he have spent just a couple of hours to make the house semi-presentable for her? Did having a wife mean nothing to him?

He walked into the room behind her and carefully placed her bags in the corner. She didn't turn to him, even though she had to know he was there. He sighed heavily. She was angry, and honestly, she had every right to be. He knew he'd messed up by not getting the cleaning done. He kept promising himself he'd find time for it, but he'd wanted to get the crops in the ground before she arrived, and he'd barely made it as it was. He was half afraid to speak to her.

"I'll uh...I'll just go and milk the cows and put the horses in the barn. I'll be back in about an hour." *Or two*, he thought to himself as he quickly left the house. He felt like he'd really been fortunate to find someone as pretty as she was to come all this way to be his wife. He hoped he hadn't messed everything up by not doing more to prepare for her.

As he unhitched the horses he found himself hoping she'd be the kind of bride he needed. Would she be willing in bed when she had to spend time just making the room clean enough to sleep in?

Maude dug through the chest of drawers in the corner of John's bedroom, slamming each drawer in turn as she searched for clean linens. Finally, she found a clean set of sheets and a pair of pillowcases. *What was wrong with him that he was willing to live in that kind of filth and not clean up after himself?* She thought wistfully about the maids she would have had as Horace's wife, and then she stilled. She could feel the way her skin crawled when Horace touched her. No, she'd made the right decision.

# Chapter Six

John tiptoed into the house an hour later, not certain what state of mind he'd find his new bride in. He stopped and stared as he walked in. She'd done up the dishes and scrubbed the table. The floors weren't clean yet, but all of the cooking and eating surfaces were. He could only assume she'd done the same in his bedroom. He smiled. For someone who looked like a perfect lady, she certainly knew how to work.

He walked through the house looking for her. She was nowhere to be seen. He climbed the stairs and found her putting her clothes away alongside his in his chest of drawers. His room had been swept and the bed was made with clean linens. The soiled clothes and bedding were nowhere to be seen. "You've been busy."

She jumped in surprise at his voice. "You startled me!"

"I'm sorry. I figured I was loud enough you'd have heard me when I came in." He smiled at her. "The house looks a lot better. I appreciate you working so hard on your wedding day."

She shook her head at him. "I couldn't live in the filth so there was really no choice. I'll give it a proper cleaning tomorrow." She turned back to her clothes and packed the last of her nightgowns into a drawer and closed it. "I'll have the house whipped into shape within a week or two." She forced a smile as she thought about the laundry that waited for her, not to mention the window washing and the hours of floor scrubbing.

"I really am sorry about the mess. My plan was to get it done, but I was late putting the crop in, and just never found the time. Will you forgive me?" He'd walked to her and took her hands in his as he asked the question.

"Of course, I forgive you. I won't start our marriage in anger." She was surprised by how soft and sweet her voice sounded. The last of her anger had faded away as she'd remembered the feel of Horace's hands on her. She couldn't be angry with the man who'd taken her out of that situation and provided her with a home.

"Thank you." His eyes met hers and he slowly lowered his head to brush his lips against hers. Her eyes fluttered closed as he moved his arms around her waist and kissed her softly. "I think I'm going to like having a wife."

Maude smiled up at him. "I'm sure I'm going to like being one."

John glanced toward the window, knowing full well it was still over an hour before dark. What would she think if he insisted he was so tired they needed to go to bed now? He almost laughed at his silly thoughts. He didn't want to wait, though. He'd thought of nothing but his wedding night since he'd first sent the letter looking for a bride. Maybe he could rush her along to bed after all. "I'm getting hungry. Will it take long to heat up the casserole for dinner?"

"I'm sorry. I didn't think. I'll run down and get it started right away." It was only six, and they'd eaten at the church supper at two, so she was surprised he was already hungry, but she hurried down the stairs and lit the fire in the stove. She'd found the cellar and had put the pot down there so it would stay chilled and not spoil.

Forty five minutes later, they sat down to an informal meal consisting of only the casserole which had been sent home from the wedding. She needed to bake some bread and churn some butter, but those things would need to wait. She hadn't even taken the time to do an inventory of the kitchen shelves yet to determine whether or not she had everything she needed.

While they ate, they chatted amiably about the area. She asked him about the crops he put in. "Mainly wheat. That's the big cash crop around here. I do a bit of corn for the livestock. We'll need to talk about whether or not you want to put in a kitchen garden, but if you do, I'll need to plow an area for you right away. It's getting too late in the year to start one."

She tilted her head to the side considering. "I do need to put in a garden, I think. That way we'll have vegetables all winter long. The cellar has plenty of shelves for storage."

"Mrs. Gunderson always put in a huge kitchen garden. She'd spend weeks and weeks canning vegetables for us."

"Do you miss her?"

He shrugged. "In a way, I do. She wasn't much of a mother to us, honestly. She was more of an employer who let us board here, but she made sure we always had plenty to eat, and had clean clothes. I can't complain, but the affection just wasn't really there." He took a bite of his food. "Al left the farm as soon as he was old enough to get a job somewhere else. He hated farming and everything that went with it. Not me, though. The first time I planted something and watched it grow, I knew I was meant to be a farmer for the rest of my life. I'm thankful the Gundersons left me this farm. I wouldn't have been able to afford one of my own. Especially not with a house like this. If not for them, I'd have brought you home to a sod house."

"You do have a beautiful home. I can't wait until I have it all cleaned and polished. It's going to be a wonderful place to raise a family." She'd finished eating and got to her feet, walking the few steps to the basin to wash the few dishes. "I'd like to send a couple of letters home on Monday if that would be okay."

"Of course! I'm sure your folks are anxious to know whether you made it here okay. I'm half surprised they didn't come with you." He shook his head. "I couldn't have let my daughter get on a train to go far away and marry some man she'd never met."

"They probably are anxious. And I promised my friend Harriett I'd send her a letter right away as well." She knew anxious was an understatement to what her parents would be feeling. Horace would have arrived home from his business trip this evening, and they would have had to try to explain her disappearance. She forced her mind away from Horace. The idea of him finding out where she was frightened her.

He brought her his plate as he finished eating, taking his seat to continue their conversation. "Harriett? The one who runs the mail order bride business? I didn't realize the two of you were friends."

"We met the day I answered your letter," she told him honestly. "We've become good friends in the time since, though. I'm going to miss her." She dried off the last of the dishes and put them away. "Do you know who this pot belongs to? I'd like to take it back when we go into town."

He shrugged. "One of the church ladies, I'm sure. We'll take it to church with us on Sunday morning and someone will claim it for her own."

She carefully set the pot at the end of the counter where it would be out of her way, but she wouldn't forget to take it back into town on Sunday morning. "I'd like to do a quick inventory of the kitchen to see what I'll need. I'm hoping there's enough that I can make it through until Monday. I need to go to town Monday anyway to mail the letters."

"That's fine. Let me get you some paper and a pencil so you can make a list." He stood and walked into the sitting area, coming back with the items for her. He resumed his seat, watching her as she carefully dug through the canisters on his counter and made notes of what she needed.

Maude had changed out of her wedding dress while he was outside seeing to the livestock. She was wearing a plain blue work dress that brought out the color of her eyes. He couldn't get over the fact that she had answered his letter for a mail order bride. What was wrong with the men out East that none of them were interested in such a beautiful woman? He certainly wasn't complaining, because he was thrilled to have found her.

Maude felt his eyes on her as she did her inventory. He had just about everything she needed in a very small quantity. She'd need to do a large shopping trip for supplies, but it could be put off until Monday morning. She was thankful she wouldn't have to run out the following day to get it done. She needed to stick close to the house to get started on the cleaning and laundry. She liked to plan things out, so she'd make herself a schedule for what cleaning she'd do on which day, but that would have to wait until she had gotten the bulk of the heavy work done.

Finally, she covered her mouth with her hand to stifle her yawn. She was tired, but wasn't in any hurry to go up to bed. She kept telling herself she'd done the right thing by coming here, but when it came right down to it, she was about to go to bed with a total stranger. Harriett had been kind enough to explain to her what happened in the marriage bed, so she didn't have any questions, but she certainly wasn't looking forward to what sounded like an uncomfortable experience.

John saw her yawn, and suggested, she make her trip to the outhouse first, and he'd wait. He was pleased to see her head straight out. He was looking forward to the coming night as much as she seemed to be dreading it.

He left to go outside when she came back into the house. She didn't say anything, and could barely look at him as she passed him. She couldn't believe how nervous she was.

She climbed the stairs and quickly changed into her nightgown. She braided her long hair into a single braid down her back so it wouldn't tangle and climbed under the covers and pulled them up to her chin. She lay on her back, wondering what he'd do if she pretended to be asleep when he got back. She took several deep breaths trying to calm herself. *It couldn't be that bad*, she thought, *or no one would do it more than once, and then they'd never have more than one child.*

She lay in the bed, staring at the ceiling waiting for John to join her. She'd hoped he'd offer her more time before consummating the marriage, but she was going to do what she'd promised to do before the pastor in church earlier that day. If he wanted to be intimate with her, then she would be intimate. He'd saved her from a life with Horrible Horace, whether he knew it or not, and she owed it to him.

John went to the barn after using the outhouse, wondering how long she'd need to get ready for bed. He had never been with a woman before and couldn't stop thinking about the beautiful woman waiting for him in his bed. He'd honestly expected to find a homely woman getting off the train and still couldn't believe his luck. Maude was the prettiest girl he'd ever seen, and he couldn't imagine a reason she would have had to resort to being a mail order bride.

He patted the neck of his black stallion, Midnight, talking to him in a low voice. "I know you've done it before, but I never have. I'm not sure I'm going to be any good at it, but I hope I don't disappoint her. Did you see how beautiful she is? I've never seen anyone like her. How long should I give her to get ready, do you think?"

Midnight snickered at him, nudging him with his nose.

"You think she's ready?" He took a deep breath. "Okay, pal, I'll trust you on this one."

He made his way slowly from the barn to the house, giving her any extra time she may need. He made certain to tread heavily as he climbed the stairs, hoping she would hear him and not be startled. The last thing he wanted to do was scare his new bride.

She was his wife, and he would cherish her in every way he could.

# Chapter Seven

John woke before sunrise the following morning as he always did. He lay on his side for a minute, with his head propped on his fist, staring at his bride. He knew she hadn't found the same pleasure in his arms he'd found in hers, and he wanted to find some way to make it up to her.

He reached out a hand and stroked her cheek, watching her eyes flutter open in the darkness. She seemed startled for a moment, but then smiled at him. "Good morning."

"Good morning. How did you sleep?"

She thought of the time she'd spent staring into the darkness after he'd gone to sleep, wishing she'd found the same elusive pleasure he had. "Okay, I guess. I've never slept in the same bed with anyone, so it was strange."

He moved closer to her, dropping a kiss on her lips. "You'll get used to it." His hand went to her braid softly stroking her hair wishing she'd left it down to sleep.

She hadn't thought about him wanting to do this often. She'd thought maybe once or twice per month to try to get her pregnant, not twice per day! His hands were all over her, sending her body humming.

Putting her arms around him, she held him close, her lips moving against his, kissing him back. If he wanted to do this again, who was she to argue? She may not have found the same kind of pleasure he had the night before, but there had been some pleasure.

A few minutes passed before he left her side and stood to get dressed. "I need to get the cows milked. It's getting light out." Once he was dressed, he leaned over the bed and kissed her softly. "Do you have any idea how incredible you are?"

She blushed. "I'll get breakfast."

"Eggs are in the henhouse." He left the room and went down the stairs to his chores whistling as he went.

Maude sat up, stripped off her nightgown, and quickly pulled on a work dress. She'd only brought two work dresses with her, one nightgown, a Sunday dress and her wedding dress. She'd need to start sewing as soon as she was finished with the house. She closed her eyes for a moment thinking about the enormous task in front of her getting the house in order.

After using the outhouse, she gathered the eggs and took them inside to cook for breakfast. It felt strange to cook for a man, but she smiled to herself. This was their first full day of marriage, and she was going to make it perfect for both of them.

BY THE END OF THE DAY she was ready to pull her hair out. She'd spent half the day washing his clothes and hanging them on the line. She'd washed all the linens in the house, made bread, fixed three meals, and scrubbed until her fingers were raw. She'd barely made a dent in the mess, and she knew she'd have to take the next day off because it was Sunday.

She'd never dreamed being a wife meant this much physical labor. Of course, her mother had always employed a maid to help around the house. She had worked in the orphanage for years, though, and should have realized all that was involved, but there were so many there to share the work it had seemed like there was less to do. She honestly didn't know how she'd handle it once children came along.

When John came in for supper, she was already yawning. She knew he'd worked hard all day, but she had worked just as hard in the house. He set the milk pail next to the basin on her worktable, and then wrapped his arms around her, kissing her neck. She tilted her head to the side to give him better access as she stirred the stew she'd made for supper. "Are you hungry?"

"Famished," he said against her neck as he nibbled contentedly.

"Well, sit down and I'll put everything on the table." She served him a big bowl of stew and several slices of bread. She got herself a bowl and sat down beside him, waiting for his prayer before she ate.

"This is delicious. You're a good cook."

"Thank you. I'm sorry I didn't have time to make anything for dessert."

He laughed. "I'm just thrilled I'm not eating my own cooking. Burnt eggs are about all I can do."

She smiled. "Well, I'm glad I saved you from a life of burnt eggs." She toyed with her stew, not very hungry, even after all the hard work she'd done. "What did you do today?"

"I had to fix a couple of fences today, and I spent a bit of time weeding the wheat field." He looked around the house noting the cleaning she'd accomplished. "You got a lot done today."

She nodded. "It's going to take me a week or two to have everything the way I want it, but I feel like I've at least gotten started."

The floor was clean enough to eat off of, and all of the laundry was dry and put away. She hadn't started on the second story yet, but was almost pleased with the first. She still wanted to get the windows washed, but that could wait until next week.

"You have a lifetime to get it done. Don't wear yourself out."

She served him a second bowl of stew and washed the dishes they'd dirtied. She felt his eyes on her as she faced away from him, looking out the window as she washed the dishes. "I made up a list of food I'll need to get from the store on Monday. I'd also like to buy some fabric for a couple of new dresses if that would be all right."

"That's fine. Don't go crazy spending all our money, but we can afford two new dresses."

She'd taken inventory of his clothes, and knew some needed mending, but he had plenty for now. "Will you go to town with me on Monday? Or should I drive myself?"

"I'll go this first time. After that you can make your way on your own." He took another bite of his stew savoring the taste. "I usually have lunch with Al and Anne on Sundays after church. Do you want to do that or come straight home?"

She thought about it for a minute. She needed to write her letters, but she had plenty of time for that. "We can go to lunch with them. I like Anne and would love to get to know her better."

He was disappointed with her answer. He would have liked to have had an entire day off with her, but he did understand her need to make friends locally. "We'll do that. Do you have anything else you need to do tomorrow?"

"I just need to write those two letters I told you about." She had been mentally composing the letter to her parents all day. She wasn't sure how to tell them what she'd done, but she didn't want them to worry about her. "I won't do any more of the heavy cleaning until Monday."

He stood to take her his dirty dishes and dropped them in the basin for her. He once again sat down and chatted with her while she finished up the dishes. He couldn't take his eyes off her. She seemed so reserved, but she certainly wasn't reserved once he got her upstairs. He smiled. She was exactly what he'd needed in his life.

# Chapter Eight

Maude was the center of attention at church on Sunday. All the women were clamoring for an introduction, and she felt more than a little overwhelmed. She'd never had a lot of friends, because her parents had kept such a tight rein on her. Even female friends had been discouraged over the years. Sure, she'd had friends at the small private school her parents had sent her to, but she'd never been allowed to see them outside of school hours, so she'd felt very much alone.

The pastor made sure to shake her hand and make her feel welcome before the sermon. She felt like she'd met half the population of Iowa by the time they sat down for the service.

After church, she was pleased when Anne took her hand and pulled her away. They walked to Anne's home with Anne chattering away animatedly. "You can just watch while I cook lunch, because I really don't need any help, and my kitchen isn't as big as yours so there's not much room for two women to be working in it." She spoke rapidly and seemed to never pause for breath. Just listening to her wore Maude out, but she was glad to not have to say much.

Maude wondered at the difference between the Anne she'd met a couple of days ago and the Anne she was with now. Maybe the first time she met someone, she had questions about them, but after that, she just preferred the sound of her own voice. Whatever it was, Maude was happy not to have to talk for a while after answering everyone's questions at the church.

"So what do you think of married life? Is John just doting on you and treating you like a queen? Please tell me he cleaned up the house before you arrived. I was going to help him, but Al said absolutely not with as far along as I am in my pregnancy. He's afraid I'm going to go into labor and give birth before he can fetch the midwife. He's really worried about the baby coming early, but I keep telling him it will all be fine." Anne never waited for an answer to anything; she seemed to just enjoy hearing her own voice asking questions whether they were answered or not.

Maude listened happily while Anne fixed lunch. She'd tried to offer to help, but Anne had cut her off mid-sentence. "Of course, you can't help. It's my house and you're my guest. Someday we'll have Sunday lunch at your house. Do you like to cook? John's favorite dessert is strawberry shortcake, and since the strawberries are ripe now, you should pick some and make it for him. There are always some growing wild on the farm. I'll give you my recipe before you go." She worked the same way she talked, rapidly without ever pausing for anything.

Once lunch was on the table, the men joined them from the front porch where they'd been talking. Anne dominated the conversation throughout the meal. As they started their dessert, Maude realized she'd never heard Al speak a single word. She wondered if that was by choice or necessity. Maybe he'd spent so long with Anne, not being allowed to speak, that he didn't remember how to carry on a conversation.

After lunch, Maude did the dishes while Anne sat and chattered away at her. "You'll have to come in sometime during the week once you're caught up on your household chores. Maybe you could come in and help me sew for the baby. We could sit and sew and just talk and talk. I love having a sister who I can talk to and share stories with, don't you?"

Maude waited a second to make sure she was really expected to answer before saying, "I do enjoy having a sister. I'm an only child, so it's nice to have someone to talk to."

"An only child? Oh, that's terrible! I mean, my brothers may have been rowdy and crazy and teasing all the time, but at least I wasn't alone. I couldn't imagine being an only child. I hope to have at least four children, so my baby won't feel all alone in the world."

When it was time to leave, Maude felt like she knew everything there was to know about Anne. She climbed onto the wagon seat next to

John and waved. "You hurry back. Don't wait until Sunday. I can't wait until we can sit down and get to know one another better without men underfoot!"

Maude just smiled, knowing by this point she wasn't expected to reply. The men had stayed on the porch the entire time except the meal anyway, but she wasn't about to point that out.

Once they were out of sight of Anne's house, Maude let out a sigh of relief. "Does she always talk that much?"

John laughed. "Always! I haven't heard Al say a word in her presence since they started courting."

Maude grinned. "They do seem like an odd couple, but that's probably why they fit together so well." She stared down at her hands for a moment. "Your brother is able to talk, isn't he?"

"Yup. Just not around her, but no one is able to talk around Anne."

They laughed together. "I need to get those letters written once we get home. Would you be okay with just having stew for dinner again tonight?" She felt guilty for even asking to make a simple meal two nights in a row, but there was so much to do. He was her husband and she wanted to spoil him with good food, but it would have to wait.

"As long as I'm not burning my own dinner, I'll eat anything!"

Once they were home, she changed out of her Sunday clothes and sat down at the table to write her letters. John sat down with a book and read while she worked on them. She wrote the letter to Harriett first, explaining she had arrived safely and that John was a kind man. She also told her the situation was better than she'd hoped for other than the state of his house.

Once she was done with Harriett's letter, she pulled another sheet of paper to her. She needed to let her parents know she was okay, but she didn't want to have to admit what she'd done. What was the best way to write it?

Finally she simply wrote, "I couldn't marry Horace. He was a bad man who frightened me. I felt if I stayed there I would have no choices in life especially once I was married to him. Instead, I replied to a letter from a man looking for a mail order bride. He's a farmer named John, and he's very kind to me. I married him on Friday. Please forgive me for the way I left. I didn't feel as if I had any other options." She signed it with love and wrote her name at the bottom.

She read over each of her letters to make certain they were saying exactly what she needed to say. Glancing at the clock, she saw it was time to start dinner if they were going to eat at a decent hour. She'd agonized over the letter to her parents for more than an hour.

John was watching her when she stood. "Are you hungry?" She wasn't sure why she was even asking. John was always hungry as far as she could tell.

He nodded. "Why don't you make something simple, though? We can just have eggs or pancakes. You don't need to go through the trouble of making a stew." He could see how upset she was and couldn't help but wonder what was in those letters. He'd thought she was simply letting her parents know she'd arrived safely.

She considered that for a moment and nodded. She was exhausted. Writing the letter to her parents had taken a lot out of her. "I'll make some pancakes." She pulled out the ingredients she'd need and a large mixing bowl.

"Do you mind if I read the letters you wrote?" He watched her face carefully for her reaction.

She started for a moment, staring at him, and then nodded slowly. She'd been looking for a way to tell him about Horace and why she'd left Beckham. She just wasn't certain how to broach the subject. This would certainly get them started talking about her decision to become his wife.

He picked up her letter to Harriett first, and she remembered too late what she'd written about the state of his house. She turned her back to him adding the ingredients and mixing the batter for the pancakes. "I'm sorry about the messy house," he said from behind her. "I should have cleaned it, but by the time I knew you were coming, it was planting season, and I was so tired at the end of every day, all I could think about was sleep. I should have paid someone to come out and do it or waited on the wedding."

She shook her head. "I understand. It was just a bit overwhelming, and Harriett needs to know that type of situation is a possibility so she can warn other women. I'm sorry I complained about you."

"You shouldn't be. This house should have been complained about." He picked up the other letter and began reading it. When he was finished, he folded it silently and sat staring at it for a minute digesting what he'd just read. "Tell me about Horace." His voice was soft, but she knew he was upset.

She poured the first of the pancakes into the frying pan. She kept her voice steady as she explained. "Horace is in his forties, and he's my father's boss. I've known him since I was a little girl. When I was about fourteen, he started looking at me in a way that made me feel uncomfortable. Over the years, he's spent more and more time at my parents' house, having dinner with us. A couple of months ago, he came to dinner, and my parents made excuses to leave us alone. He asked me to marry him, and when I told him 'no', he told me I didn't have a choice." She took a deep shaky breath, putting the first of the pancakes on a plate and handing them to him before she continued. "He kissed me and touched me, and it made me feel like there were spiders crawling all over me. It was horrible."

John stared down at the food in front of him, reaching for the molasses she'd set on the table. "Why didn't you tell your parents that?"

She poured more pancakes. "I did. They told me he'd provide well for me." She looked out the window for a moment. "He had enough money to provide well. That was the truth. But he would have been cruel to me. I was so afraid of him." Putting the pancakes on a plate, she carried them to the table, forking two of the four onto his plate, before settling down with her own. "I overheard Harriett talking at the post office about not having enough brides for all the letters she was receiving less than a week later. I jumped at the chance. I sneaked out in the middle of the night to take my bags to Harriett, so I could just leave for the train without it being obvious. My parents thought I went to the orphanage to work that morning, and they haven't seen me since."

"I'm sure they're worried sick." He couldn't imagine how he would feel if his daughter went off to work one morning and simply never returned. He was certain they were in a state of terror.

"I know. I feel terrible about it. I just didn't know what else to do."

He reached across the table and took her hand in his. "You did the right thing. I wish you'd told me, but you shouldn't have stayed in that situation."

She met his eyes for the first time since he'd read the letters. "I didn't want you to think I was a bad person for running away and marrying you when I was engaged to someone else."

He shook his head. "You never agreed to marry the man, so engaged or not, you weren't committed to him. I'm glad you're my wife."

"I am too." And she was. When she'd left Beckham, she had been frightened and worried every time she'd seen someone move behind her. Here, she felt free. She'd married a good man, and she knew they'd have a good life together.

After making love that night, he held her close for a long time staring up at the dark ceiling. He was sorry circumstances had forced her to marry, but so glad she'd married him. She slept with her head pillowed on his shoulder, and he dropped a kiss on top of it. He was going to make sure she never had any regrets about deciding to be his wife.

# Chapter Nine

John was proud to walk into the general store in town the following morning with Maude on his arm. He introduced her to the shopkeeper and the other people they ran into. She carefully chose her selections, mainly buying food. When she had left a pile of items on the counter, she wandered over to the selection of dry goods.

John followed her, watching as she carefully checked the quality and price of each bolt of cloth. "I need something that will hold up well for the chores I'll be doing, but won't cost us too dearly."

John smiled at her. "Pick what you like and let me worry about the cost. I'm not rich, but I do have some money saved."

She shook her head. "You saved the money for a rainy day. The sun is shining right now." She picked up a bolt of cloth and checked the price. "This will be perfect to make some aprons from. I don't have one, and I'm definitely going to need some if I don't want all my dresses soiled." She handed him the bolt to hold while she looked for other fabrics.

She chose two more for summer dresses. She'd need to make some dresses for winter when the time came, but two would be enough for now. She bought thread and some needles as well, carrying those to the front while John carried the fabric.

"That's a lot of sewing you're going to be doing there, Mrs. Powers."

She smiled. "I only have city dresses, and I'll need some that will be good for doing chores around the farm." The fabrics she'd picked were not the prettiest, as she would have chosen in Beckham, but they were the sturdiest and least expensive.

"These will be perfect for summer dresses." He quickly tallied the order for the food and the fabric. He named a price that had Maude ready to put some things back, but John shook his head and paid for it all. "Thanks, Mr. Green."

Mr. Green smiled. "It's my pleasure. I'll see you Sunday!"

Maude waited while John put everything into the bed of the wagon. "Are you sure we didn't spend too much?"

John shook his head. "You were very careful with your purchases. Is there anything there we don't need?" With the way she'd debated over every purchase, he knew there wasn't but he had to make her see that.

She thought about it for a moment. "Well, no, but I could wait for a bit on the dresses if I needed to."

"You don't need to. You need new dresses, and you're going to get them." He squeezed her hand as he drove. "So, what are you going to do for the rest of the day?"

It was only eleven in the morning as they headed back out toward the farm. "I thought maybe I'd fix you some lunch, since you seem to be hungry all the time," she teased. "Then I need to clean the second story of the house. All of the linens in the spare rooms need to be cleaned, but I'll do that on laundry day. I'll at least get the floors scrubbed and clean. I want to scrub the parlor floor." She paused smiling at him. "Then, depending on the time, I'll either cook or start on one of the aprons. I need them more than I need dresses."

"Wow. I'm just going to weed the wheat field. You make me feel positively lazy." He turned and gave her a slow wink.

She laughed. "We both have our chores to keep us busy."

"Think you can squeeze in time to make dessert tonight?" He'd been eyeing some wild strawberries that were on the east side of the property. "I'll bring some fresh strawberries when I come in for supper."

She grinned. She'd been planning to bake a cake for dessert anyway. "Strawberry shortcake?"

He nodded. "It's my favorite."

"Then I'll make the cake and you bring the strawberries. It won't take any time at all to sweeten them for the topping." She liked the idea of baking special treats for him. She was happy to be married to someone she liked, who she would want to do things for instead of Horace. She did her best to block him out of her mind. They'd mailed her letters off that morning, and she knew she'd be hearing back within a month or so. If her parents were still willing to speak to her, of course.

She finished her chores earlier than she'd expected that afternoon, so began sewing her apron. She had worn them working at the orphanage, of course, but there had really never been a need for her to wear them at home. Their maid, Sally, had done all of the cleaning in her home.

# Chapter Ten

It took her a full two weeks to get the house how she wanted it. After the crops were in, she hoped to have a bit of money left over to make new curtains, but that was her only complaint about the house.

Their days fell into an easy pattern. She made breakfast while he milked the cows and fed the animals. Then he went off to work in the fields while she took care of the house.

On the day she finally felt caught up, she made his favorite meal, chicken and dumplings, to celebrate and made him another strawberry shortcake. She planned on spending a couple of hours the next day to go out and pick strawberries so she could preserve them. They'd be out of season in another week, and she didn't want them to go to waste.

After their prayer, he smiled down at his plate. "You made my favorites!"

She grinned. "I finally got caught up on the chores, so I have more time now. I can make better meals and spend more time on my dresses. I'm going to go out and pick all the strawberries tomorrow."

"Sounds good to me! Are you making jam?"

She nodded. "I know how much you love strawberries. I'll make as much as I can."

"There are canning supplies down in the cellar."

"I know. I've already washed out all the jars so I'm ready to go." She paused, her spoon halfway to her mouth. "Do you think it would be okay to invite Anne out here to help me? I've never made jam before, and I'd love to get her advice."

"Of course! Why don't you ride into town in the morning and invite her out for Wednesday? You can get everything picked tomorrow, and then you can make the jam with her then?"

"I've never driven a wagon."

He grinned. "It's easy. I'll hitch up the team after breakfast, and we'll drive around for a few minutes. That way you'll feel comfortable when you go." He squeezed her hand tightly. "I'm glad you're becoming friends with Anne. She's really close to her family but doesn't have a lot of friends otherwise. She needs a good female friend."

"It's hard to believe she doesn't have a lot of friends. She's so easy to be around."

"Only for shy people. You like her because you're a little timid around new people. Anyone who actually likes to answer questions asked of them gets frustrated with her pretty quick."

Maude laughed. "That's not very nice."

"But it is true." Maude found she couldn't argue with that.

TRUE TO HIS WORD, IMMEDIATELY after breakfast the following morning, John spent thirty minutes teaching Maude how to drive the team. They drove up and down the dirt road and then out onto the main road that led into town. "Hold your hands steady now. They need to know someone has a firm hold on them."

Maude was nervous and holding on for dear life. "I'm not sure I'm ready to drive all the way into town!"

"We'll practice a little more, and then you'll be ready to go." His hand dropped to her knee squeezing it reassuringly. "Our team is gentle and won't run off. You'll be fine."

An hour later, a much calmer Maude made her way into town. She stopped in front of Al and Anne's house and walked up to the door knocking softly.

Anne came to the door with flour all over her hands. "Maude! Come in. I was just doing the day's baking."

Maude followed Anne into the kitchen and sat down at the table. "I can't stay long, but I wanted to come and see if you'd come out to the farm tomorrow to help me make strawberry preserves. We have so many strawberries even John's sweet tooth can't eat them all."

Anne nodded. "I'd love to! What time?"

Maude shrugged. "I've already washed the jars, and I'm going to spend this afternoon picking the strawberries and washing them. Whenever you come, we'll get started. I've never made jam, so I need your help if you don't mind."

"I need to get out of this house and quit worrying about the baby."

"Why are you worried? Is something wrong?" Maude was surprised by how much Anne had let her talk this morning. She really wasn't acting like herself.

"Nothing's wrong, I've just never given birth before, so I'm worried about the delivery, and I'm worried that I won't be a good mother, and I'm worried that we won't have enough money, and what would happen if I were to die in childbirth? Who would take care of the baby? And what if I don't drop the weight I put on during my pregnancy? Will Al still love me? And what if my baby is so ugly no one can stand to look at her? What if it's a boy and so puny he can't do any chores?"

Maude found herself chuckling. Anne really did need to get away from her own thoughts for a while. She stood and hugged her sister in law tightly. "I need to go back to the farm, but everything is going to be fine. I'll see you tomorrow, okay?"

Anne nodded laughing at herself. "I'll be there after I finish the breakfast dishes. Would that be okay?"

"Absolutely. I'll see you then."

As Maude drove home, she was shaking her head and chuckling at all the crazy thoughts going through Anne's mind. It was like everyone in the world moved at a slow pace, and Anne didn't have a slow bone in her body. She was glad she'd decided to ask her new friend to join her for making jam, not only because she needed help, but because it would be a welcome respite from her own company for Anne.

She went to the basement and found two large metal pails to use for picking strawberries. Putting on her oldest dress, one she'd worn for working at the orphanage back in Beckham, she walked happily out to the wild strawberry patch. As she picked the berries she hummed softly, happy to be able to choose what she would do every day with no one watching over her shoulder every minute.

She was halfway through filling up her second pail, when she felt two arms wrap around her waist and a mouth nibbling at her neck. She giggled and turned into John's arms lifting her lips for his kiss. "Why aren't you working?"

He shrugged. "I was working in the field not twenty feet from here, and you never even noticed me. I figured if my new bride didn't notice me, I must be doing something wrong."

She put her pail down and looped her arms around his neck. "What could my wonderful husband possibly think he's doing wrong? I was just thinking about how good life is now."

"You're not sorry you gave up life with your rich man to come here and be a farmer's wife?"

She looked into his green eyes. "You're really worried about that? I would do it again in a heartbeat. I'm happy here." She couldn't believe how happy she was. She'd married a good man who liked her a great deal, even if he didn't love her. As stared into his eyes, she realized that he was what had made her so happy. Yes, she was thrilled to have escaped Horace, but John made her want to sing through her work every day. She loved him.

"I'm glad." His voice was a mere whisper as he leaned down to brush her lips with his. "I'm so happy you're here....although you do keep distracting me from my work. How am I supposed to make a living if you keep dragging me out of the wheat field to kiss me?"

She laughed. "I don't guess we could get anyone to pay us for kissing, could we?"

"I really don't think so." He sounded let down at the reality of their situation. To be paid to kiss his wife would have been heaven.

"We'll have to hurry up and have children, so they can work in the wheat field while you and I stay in the house and kiss, then."

He tilted his head to the side as if considering the idea. "Not a bad suggestion. Let's get to work on that right now."

She blushed bright red. "It's the middle of the day! Go back to your wheat and let me pick strawberries."

He sighed. "Thwarted by the sun. If it were raining?"

"I'm married to a crazy man."

He made a show of reluctance as he turned to head back to his wheat field dragging his feet the whole way. "At least I'll see you at lunchtime."

She grinned at his silliness. "Lunch will be in an hour. Be on time or I'll eat your share myself." She watched him walk away before picking up her half full pail of berries.

# Chapter Eleven

When Anne arrived the following morning, Maude had all of the strawberries washed and the stems picked out. Anne quickly explained the process of making the jam and canning it in the jars, and then proceeded to spend the morning talking about her fears for the baby. Maude sincerely hoped her mind didn't disappear when she became pregnant, but judging by Anne, there was a good chance of it.

They were able to put up thirty jars of strawberry jam by the end of the day. Maude had sent a lunch pail with John to the field that morning so he wouldn't have to see the mess she knew they'd make. She enjoyed working with a friend beside her.

Anne left in late afternoon with ten jars of jam. Maude carefully carried the rest down the stairs and put them on the shelves lining the walls, keeping one in the kitchen to put on the bread she'd serve with their dinner.

At dinner, she broached the next project she wanted to start. "I need to put in a kitchen garden. Can you spare the time to plow a section of the yard for me?"

"Sure. It's getting in late, but I think it will still grow. I'll do that in the morning. Do you have the seed you need for it?"

She shook her head. "No, I'll need to go to the store. Would you hitch up the team for me to go in the morning while you're plowing?"

"Of course."

After dinner, he went to the bedroom and brought down some money for her. "This will be enough to buy what you need."

She looked at the money in her hand. She'd never bought seed, but it looked like it would be more than enough to her.

While she was in town, she asked if she'd received any letters, but nothing had come for her yet. She was looking forward to hearing from Harriett, but dreading a return letter from her parents. Not enough time had passed for a letter to come for her, but she hoped one would be there soon.

She spent the afternoon planting her seeds in straight rows. When she was finished, she stood, rubbing her back. Looking down at herself, she saw she was covered with dirt, and she had to laugh. If people back home could see her like that, they would be shocked.

It was three days later when she was out watering her garden that she saw a figure riding toward them on a horse. He was riding fast and she watched as he approached, wondering who it was.

As he got closer, she realized it was Horace. Her parents must have told him where she was. She took a deep breath and closed her eyes, afraid to talk to him, but having no choice. John was too far away to hear her if she screamed. She'd need to deal with him on her own.

He stopped the horse and dismounted, standing in front of her with a mad look on his face. "Pack your things. You're coming home with me."

She shook her head. "No, I'm not. I'm a married woman now. I can't leave my husband and go back to Beckham. I'm happy here." *So much happier than I ever could have been with you.*

"How can you be happy working in the fields like a common laborer? You're a lady, and you belong with me!" Spit sprayed from his mouth as he yelled the words at her. His face was red with anger.

"I'm married to a man I love. All the money in the world couldn't make me any happier than I am right now." Her words were spoken softly but passionately. The look in her eyes left no doubt that she was speaking the truth.

Horace shook his head. "That's not true!" He took a step toward her and grabbed her arm.

"Let her go." She saw John walking up behind him with his rifle in his hands. The rifle was aimed at the back of Horace's head. "I have a gun, and I will use it on you if you don't let my wife go."

Horace dropped her arm and spun around to face John. "She's mine! I bought her lock stock and barrel! I paid for her private all-girls school. I've paid for everything she's worn since she was fourteen with the understanding she would be married to me as soon as she was old enough. Her parents stalled, but they finally agreed she was ready. So she's mine."

Maude's eyes widened at Horace's words. She prayed they weren't true. Would her parents really have all but sold her to him?

"That doesn't make her yours. She married me, and the ring on her finger makes her mine. Her last name is Powers now. That makes her mine." John kept his rifle trained at Horace's head as he spoke in a soft even voice. Maude had no doubt that he would protect her with his life.

"I paid for her! I gave her father thousands of dollars in bonuses so she would marry me!"

John sighed. "She's mine. Get off my property. You're trespassing, and that gives me the right to shoot you. Go, and don't come back."

Horace glared at him, but got back onto his horse. "I'm not giving up on her."

John kept the gun pointed at Horace's head as he rode away. Once he was out of sight, he carefully rested the rifle against a tree, and held his arms out for Maude who ran into them. "Now I understand."

"Thank you! What are we going to do, though? He's going to come back. I know he will. You can't always be with me."

John held her close while he thought about the answer. "I'm going to teach you to shoot a pistol. You need to sew a pocket on your aprons and keep the pistol in your pocket at all times." He finally let her go enough that he could look down into her eyes. "Okay?"

She nodded. "When do you want to start?"

He took her hand and led her to the barn. "We'll start now. There's no telling when that madman will be back."

# Chapter Twelve

For hours they practiced shooting at a target until Maude's hands were shaking too badly to hold the gun steady any longer. "Let's go into town this evening and check on Anne. Her time is close, and I want to talk to Al, anyway."

Maude was surprised, but nodded her agreement. She gathered a loaf of the fresh bread she'd made that morning and the cake she'd made for dessert. She knew that whatever Anne was serving for dinner would be more than enough with those two additions.

They arrived as Anne was putting dinner on the table. She immediately invited them to sit down. "Eat with us!"

"I brought bread and strawberry shortcake to supplement," Maude offered. She didn't feel as guilty about invading during their dinner time when she had food to share.

"Thank you. Sit down." Anne guided Maude toward the table as she went to get more dishes for her unexpected guests. When she came back, she smiled at Maude. "Did you see your father? He came by today asking about you."

Maude's eyes met John's. "My father? An overweight man with dark hair around forty? Red face who spits when he talks?"

"That's him! He said he missed you and he came all this way to visit. I'm surprised he didn't come into town with you." Anne seemed genuinely happy her friend's father had come into town unexpectedly.

"Did you give him directions out to our place?" John asked with a mild voice.

"Yes, of course. I knew Maude would be excited to see him."

"That wasn't her father. That man is the reason Maude left her town and married me. He was trying to force her to marry him. He came to the farm today and threatened her." His eyes met Al's. "I need her to stay with you while I go see the sheriff."

Al nodded quickly. "Of course."

Maude looked at Al in surprise. She'd never heard the man speak before. After a moment she turned to John. "I don't want you going alone! He's angry with you, too!"

Al tipped his head to the side looking at Anne. After a moment Anne spoke. "I'm a crack shot. Al can go with John, and Maude can stay here with me."

Maude's eyes widened. "You can shoot, Anne? You seem so ladylike."

Anne blushed looking down at her food. "I grew up with brothers. They had no respect for me because I couldn't outdo them at anything physical. So, I learned to shoot. I never miss."

Al nodded agreeing with Anne. "I've seen her. I've never seen another man or woman who can shoot as straight as my Annie." His voice was filled with pride as he talked about her achievements.

John looked from Al to Anne. "Are you serious?" He couldn't believe he'd known Anne for three years, but had never known that about her.

Anne nodded. "It's not exactly something I want to be known for, though, so let's not talk about it anymore. You two go, and Maude will stay here with me. We'll be safe without you."

Immediately after dinner, the men rode off to speak with the sheriff. "Be careful while we're gone," John told Maude. "You ladies need to keep the door shut and keep your guns at the ready at all times." He turned to his brother who was admonishing Anne in the same way. "You ready?"

Maude and Anne went into the kitchen to do the dishes. Once they were finished, they sat sewing on a quilt Anne was making for the baby. "I hope the men hurry back," Anne finally said after several minutes of silence.

Maude nodded. "I don't like them being out alone at night knowing he's around here somewhere just waiting." She shivered slightly as she thought about what could happen to the men.

"I'm glad you didn't marry him and came out here instead. I can't imagine John being nearly as happy with anyone else."

"Being married to Horace would have been no life at all. I did the right thing by leaving, but I just hope he doesn't take it out on my parents. My father's worked for him since before I was born."

Anne looked at Maude intently. "Why would you be worried about them when they sold you for all intents and purposes?"

Maude shrugged and looked down at the block she was quilting. "I guess because they're my parents, and in their own way, they love me."

"If you say so." She looked at the clock again. "They should be back any minute." Anne heard a sound from outside and ran to the door throwing it open. She immediately tried to slam it shut again, but was too late.

Horace pushed her to the floor, his eyes roaming the room for Maude, who was still sitting on the couch, with the quilt covering her lap. "There you are. What are you going to do now that your husband isn't here to protect you?"

Maude ignored Horace, knowing she couldn't go for her gun with his own pistol pointed at her. "Anne, are you okay?"

"I think so. What kind of man knocks down a pregnant woman? What is wrong with him?"

JOHN AND AL RODE QUICKLY through the small town with the sheriff, Tom Bennigan, between them. They stopped in front of Al's house, and saw the door standing open. Immediately all three men went on alert.

The sheriff, without speaking, motioned John to go around the back one way, and for Al to go the other. He carefully walked toward the house with his gun drawn, aimed at the intruder. "I'm the sheriff and I'm going to need you to drop your gun, mister. Put it on the floor slowly, and keep your hands where I can see them."

Horace spun in the direction of the sheriff, his gun still raised, and aimed for Tom's chest.

The sheriff didn't hesitate as he pulled the trigger, his bullet sinking into Horace and killing him instantly. He ran into the house to make sure he was dead, before calling to the other men all was clear. John and Al burst through the back door, and each man ran to his wife.

Al dropped to his knees beside Anne. "Are you okay? Did he hurt you?"

Anne was shaking as she answered. "He just knocked me down. I don't think I'm hurt; I just didn't want to move with that gun in his hand. He seemed a little too trigger happy for my tastes." She kept her eyes fixed on her husband's face so she wouldn't have to look at the man lying dead on her living room floor.

The sheriff dropped down next to Maude on the couch. "I need you to tell me everything, Mrs. Powers. I need to know what happened back in Massachusetts and what's happened here."

John knelt on the floor in front of Maude, holding her hand in his as she explained everything she knew about the situation to the sheriff. Finally, the sheriff nodded and got to his feet. "Would you men mind helping me get him out of here? We'll need to give him a decent burial, whether he deserves it or not." He looked at Maude. "Do you need to telegraph your parents about the situation so his affairs can be seen to?"

Maude nodded. "I probably do." She clung to John's hand, not wanting to let go. "Where is the telegraph office?"

"It's next to the general store. Why don't you just write out what you want to say, and I'll see to it in the morning?" Tom waited as John and Al got to their feet. "It's going to take all three of us to get him out of here. Let's take him to the doc so he can get him ready to go in the ground."

Maude and Anne sat staring at one another while the men carried him out the door. Maude stared at the pool of blood on the hardwood floor of her friend's home. "Let me get that clean for you. You need to sit and rest." She helped Anne up off the floor and went to the kitchen to get a rag to clean up the mess.

IT WAS MUCH LATER THAT Maude and John were able to go home in their wagon. Maude had taken care of Anne until the men returned, but as soon as John was with her again, she started shaking.

Once they were home, they readied for bed, Maude still in shock over the events of the evening. "I'm so sorry I brought this out here with me," she whispered softly to John once they were lying in bed together.

"You didn't cause this. The only person to blame here is Horace, and maybe your parents to a lesser extent." He stroked his hand over her hair over and over. "Are you okay?"

She nodded. "In a way I'm glad it happened. I'd have spent my whole life looking over my shoulder for him. He was crazy."

"He was. I lost ten years of my life when I saw the door standing open with him pointing a gun at you." He hugged her closer. "What would I have done if I'd lost you? I love you, Maude."

She smiled against his shoulder. "I love you, too. I've wanted to tell you for days, but I just wasn't sure how."

"The simplest way is just to open up your mouth and say the words."

She propped herself up on her elbow and looked down at him in the darkness. "I love you."

He gathered her close once more, kissing her cheek. "I'm so glad you picked my letter."

"Me too. Who'd have ever thought I'd be a mail order bride?"

A MONTH LATER A LARGE crate arrived for Maude. She had picked it up when she went into town for their supplies. She waited until John was in from the fields for the evening, and asked him if he'd bring it in for her. She was certain it must be from her parents.

John carried the crate in and set it on the floor next to the table, carefully opening it with his hammer. Maude stood next to him peering inside. She'd yet to hear from her parents, and hoped to find a letter in among whatever else her parents had sent.

On top of all of her clothes was a letter in her mother's hand. Maude took it to the table and opened it immediately. "My dear Maude, I'm so sorry about trying to force you to marry Mr. Templeton. He approached your father with the idea of marrying you when you were only fourteen. Your father kept putting him off, but he made it clear your father would be fired if he didn't give in. Finally, we couldn't put him off any longer without your father losing his job. Please forgive us. We've sent your things on to you and are thrilled you've found a good man. Please write often. Your loving mother."

Maude had tears in her eyes as she lifted them to John's. "He was forcing them to make me marry him. They do love me."

John took the seat next to Maude's and hugged her tightly. "Of course, they do. How could anyone help but love you?"